# Cat in a Bag

Written by Roderick Hunt

Illustrated by Nick Schon,
based on the original characters
created by Alex Brychta

OXFORD
UNIVERSITY PRESS

**Read these words**

in     cat

bag     tin

hat     had

tub     tap

Wilf had a cat.

He put a hat on the cat.

Wilf had a bag.

He put the cat in the bag.

tap, tap, tap

7

Wilf had a tub.

He put the bag in the tub.

tap, tap, tap

9

Wilf had a tin.

He put the tub in the tin.

tap, tap, tap

11

Wilf had the cat in his hat.

# Missing letters

Choose the letter to make the word.

c _ t

W _ lf

t _ n

h _ t

13

## Talk about the story

What did Wilf put on the cat?

Why was Wilf dressed up?

How did the cat get on top of Wilf's head?

What magic trick would you like to do?

# Match the words to things you can find in the picture

Point to the ones you can find.

Wilf         tub         bag

tin         cat         hat

# It

Written by Roderick Hunt

Illustrated by Nick Schon,
based on the original characters
created by Alex Brychta

OXFORD
UNIVERSITY PRESS

**Read these words**

him          Mum

hit          rug

fit          but

did          mud

Chip was "it".

He put on the cap.

Mum ran and Kipper ran.

Mum got on the box.

Kipper got on the rug.

Biff ran.

She got on the box.

Dad ran, but Chip got him.

Dad put on the cap.
It did not fit.

Bam! Dad ran into Floppy.

Dad hit the mud.

# Missing letters

Choose the letter to make the word.

b _ x          r _ g

m _ d          l _ g

## Talk about the story

What game was the family playing?

Which people were "it"?

Why did Dad call Floppy a 'Bad dog'?

What games do you like to play?

# Match the words to things you can find in the picture

Point to the ones you can find.

box     on     dog     mud

Mum     log     rug     run

# How many words can you find with *a, o, i* or *u* in them?

Can you write them down?

| | | | | |
|---|---|---|---|---|
| c | a | t | i | n |
| o | r | u | g | u |
| p | i | l | o | g |
| b | o | x | i | p |
| t | a | h | i | m |